T0132413

Housewife

AMRITA MUKHERJEE

AuthorHouse™
1663 Liberty Drive
Bloomington, IN 47403
www.authorhouse.com
Phone: 1 (800) 839-8640

Published by AuthorHouse 06/28/2017

ISBN: 978-1-5246-9786-0 (sc)
ISBN: 978-1-5246-9787-7 (e)

Library of Congress Control Number: 2017910217

Print information available on the last page.

Any people depicted in stock imagery provided by Thinkstock are models,
and such images are being used for illustrative purposes only.
Certain stock imagery © Thinkstock.

This book is printed on acid-free paper.

Because of the dynamic nature of the Internet, any web addresses or links contained in this book may have changed
since publication and may no longer be valid. The views expressed in this work are solely those of the author and do not
necessarily reflect the views of the publisher, and the publisher hereby disclaims any responsibility for them.

authorHOUSE®

Dedicated to my MOM
Purnima Mukherjee

Dedicated to my DAD
Satyabrata Mukherjee

Dedicated to my husband
Aniket Bhattacharya

Contents

Chapter 1

Devika stirred reluctantly in bed. Alarm was buzzing. It's ruthless Monday morning. The whole universe will fall apart if she snuggles few more minutes in bed. Still, she did not force herself out. She was smoothly folded in that precious dream of her. In Calcutta, in front of Presidency portico..... giggling with friends on the staircase, ...lazy afternoon rolling peacefully under huge Krishnachura tree with convulsive red flowers, faint sound of Streetcars, ... smell of deep fried kachuri floating in ethereal air, those moments of unbelievable fun and fearless innocent gossiping with friends…she was dipping her finger in kuler chutney… slpshhhhhuplps.......tinkering with tongue twistfully.....and licking. All of a sudden something heavy, wet and soggy dropped on her face.

"Goddammn it Devi what the f…. is wrong with you? Can't you move? Move your lazy ass babe ITS MONDAYYYY….." Sanjay's voice blurted through the bathroom door.

The wet towel was thrown to the bed. "Where are my shirts? This one? With two buttons missing? Nice work. SERIOUSLY? I am going to sit in that bloody meeting with open chest showing my sexy hair to the boss? What's your problem?. What do you do all day?…HUH? My foot……a damn lazy housewife. Can't even fix two buttons in the shirt. I told you to pack my suitcase since Friday. I travel twice a week. This bloody job, the pressure…….don't you get it? "

Devika sat up quickly. She removed the towel from her face. Her Monday begun.

Chapter 2

Platoon did not want cornflakes. He wanted toast and butter like Daddy. He poured the half bottle of syrup in the bowl and started yelling "mommy! it's wacky….awww…goooeyyy ….I don't want it".

Sanjay looked at Platoon's plate as he was swiping his own silver on the plate loudly…something Devika hates with all her guts. A creepy screech that reverberates every last nerve of her body.

"Why do you give him impractical food in the morning when we all are rushing?"

She did not reply.

Sanjay continued "How'd you know? You stay home all day; fancy in your appetite…..we had to run". She did not remind him that platoon's pediatrician recommended cornflakes at morning as he was steadily gaining weight on toast, sausage, egg diet.

With a speed of missile she packed the lunch, washed all dishes, dressed Platoon, matched the socks, signed the homework folder, got ready, filled the water bottle and got down to garage.

She was fastening seatbelt, Platoon slammed the door "Wait Mommy; I forgot my science project"…..awkwardly getting out of car. Sanjay yelled. "I got to go to airport! idiot !!!…… hurry up….Devi !!! I forgot to print boarding pass."

She took his phone and retraced his flight from her email and found the boarding pass saved it on his android screen. Finally all in board, she was driving safely in the neighborhood. She dropped Platoon at the bus stop and sped thru 695 US highway to be on time at the domestic terminal. Sanjay kept returning office phone calls while in car and ran to the gate without saying any goodbye and forgetting unnecessary kisses.

On her way she stopped at Dunkins Donut and got herself a cup of coffee. Sat few min quietly in her car. Some precious independent moments of a lonely housewife.

She never imagined herself like being this when she was a nineteen year old strong head political science honors at Presidency. She looked in the semi dirty car mirror which reflects a bored, docile face with mild wrinkles of constant worries in the fore head and corners of two almond shaped brown, lucid eyes.

No spark of excitement left in those eyes which were famous in her coffee house days while vehemently arguing about all impractical topics of theoretical politics with her classmates. Lohit used to tease her " Arre baapre...chokh diye agun beroy tor". When she had to agree for her parent-conspired typical NRI marriage, Lohit laughed a lot. "We will save your spot in the corner coffee house table. That NRI MAAL is going to return you in two weeks. If you keep giving those fiery looks."

He was wrong. She stayed for last eight years now in USA. She does not remember anymore what she was all excited and argued all the time those days. These days she is an expert coupon saver, Rosmalai maker and good Mom who knows how to make party decoration with white fluffy party napkins and foam plates.

She wears false eyelashes in special parties, eyeliner even for next door grocery store while buying milk and push up wired bra, even though totally unnecessary considering her full ripe figure. She has ninety three semi-preciouses, silk based, sequined or embroidered saris and three tall jewelry cases full spectacular varieties of gold and contemporary junk sets. She drives a midsize luxury SUV Audi and living in a moderately priced two storied townhouse. In the process of getting all these she lost those sparks in her eyes.

That had no use in her now tranquil comfortable family cocoon.

However, she still drinks coffee whenever she feels down like today. ....

Chapter 3

She restarted the engine unwillingly. She has to go back home now. Tons of laundry needed to be done. Had to pick up vegetables from KROGER. May be a trip to Fish market for new batch of Shad announced to be arrived last week, which reminds Samrat the much coveted taste of Hilsa in Calcutta. She parked her car under shade in the common parking lot and was walking to the front entrance of her town home.

Suddenly she saw her coming. A short dark woman….looks like desi…. wearing a loose dirty pink house coat and floppy slipper… she was running like a floating pillow case….and almost stumbled on her… saying inconsistent…

"HELP HELP"…half shouts, delirious shiver mixed shouts…

"Please help…my husband…is dying….very sick… I AM NEW here…yes I am from India…. ANDHRA…Please call somebody…he is rolling his eye….I DON'T KNOW what to do……I have a little baby girl……MAM…please help me"

…..she was shaking…..hair mixed with saliva on face….eyes are protruding…… .

Devika dropped everything on grass…started running and calling 911 on her cell…… following the hysteric unknown Andhra girl. It was the town house behind them…door ajar… on the first level living room sofa…a midsize dark man was having full convulsive seizure. Eyes were rolling with jerking tonic clonic movements, white frothy fluid gushing out of the corners of the swelled pale lips…an animal like moaning sounds filled the small room and a little girl clutching the portico door with complete horror stricken face…crying feebly occasionally …

"Daddy…Daddy don't do that. I am scared."

Devika did not think much…..ran to the kitchen and slammed the freezer door open as she grabbed two ice trays …whacked them on counter top ….cubes burst out with rage.

She wrapped cold ice cubes in a paper towel and hold like a makeshift ice bag around his shaking head. His moaning became violent as she could hear the sirens…EMS van pulled in front of the building and three tall men with black box ran inside.

They put valium shot and started EKG as he was phasing out. Devika hold the little girl in her lap tightly as the poor thing was shaking uncontrollably with shock and fear. Tear rolling down on sweet plum like cheeks. Within minutes, EMS men quickly assessed him and wrapped him in a mobile stretcher and loaded him in the VAN. The Tallest guy with blue eyes told Devika that they are taking him at the regional lakeside ER. She must follow with the wife to get more updates.

He spoke in a solemn voice that it seems like more complicated than a mere seizure or stroke. Something that he does not see every day.

Chapter 4

On their way to hospital Devika gathered rest of the story. The woman's name is Malika. Her husband is from Andhra Pradesh in India. She is actually a Telugu Brahmin who came only two weeks ago to USA to join her husband who is a software engineer in some indo American collaboration company. Her husband Rudra Panth is only 32 year of age, from a remote village of Andhra, only person from his village who could make to Chennai IIT.

They were married three years ago. Have a baby girl of age two, Rumelia. Rudra got a lucrative transfer offer to come USA one year ago and came alone to settle himself. Visa processing took some time, so Malika with baby girl joined him only fifteen days ago fresh from India. Malika, as a girl, went to a local Chennai merthamaid convent school so she can speak English. She knows how to run dishwasher and microwave and just learned how to operate the four burners stove.

Today Rudra took a day off from office and was having tea while seating on sofa and watching TV with Rumelia. Malika was in the kitchen and suddenly she heard the moaning sound and ran to the living room and found her husband's tongue is hanging out of the face and eyes rolled up. She tried to wake him up and he started choking and hiccupping. She got confused and terrified. She did not know how to call rescue so ran outside desperately even leaving the girl alone. God was in her favor as she believes how she found Devika in the parking lot.

The ER was in regular pandemonium as usual. Two gunshot wounds victim dripping blood all over the place came in with whirlwind speed and yelling family members.

The nurse was howling to keep people out of the ICU. A black lady was slurring vicious cursing to everybody as no body pay no attention to her private abscess.

Few scared Chinese ladies were huddled in the corner as a red eyed, crumpled white coat cladded tired resident doctor was trying to explain hepatitis C is not as bad as HIV.

Devika hold Malika's hand tight and weaved through the insane misery of typical ER frantic illnesses and came close to ICU. The nurse was kind enough to give them a makeshift chair at least to seat one person. Malika sat uncomfortably with sleeping Rumelia in the lap in that rickety chair as it creaked with weight.

Chapter 5

After 25 unbearable minutes, Doctor Martin came out thru the glass door. He directly spoke to Devika assuming Malika is a non-English speaking entity.

His polished manners were not good enough to cover the cut and dry way of communication. He uttered in a silky note "YOU MUST BE FAMILY ? Hello ! this is Dr. Martin, nice to meet you. I am afraid he is having Gullian Burre Syndrome, a strange neurological disorder, can cause upward paralysis and gradual crippling of muscular system. Generally starts as a side effect of viral fever or FLU.

Did he have FLU recently?"

Malika nodded yes.

He looked surprised; acknowledging the transparency of a stolid looking South East Asian dark woman. He nodded sadly. "I am not seeing much prospect of any fast recovery. I called stat neurological consult. They are the people will have better answer for you. There is no point of you waiting here with the child. Please go home. You will be contacted".

He took slow, thoughtful stride through the maddening crowd of the ER and was lost soon like last hope.

Devika shivered inside with a raw, naked anxiety. Malika stood up and with two big tearful eyes spoke softly to Devika " DIDI(Dear Sister), I don't believe the doctor. MY HUSBAND WILL BE FINE."

Chapter 6

Platoon was not happy first. He whispered semi-audibly "Mom !!! Who is that tiny baby girl in the back seat ?....I don't like her....I hate her.....why is she in our car ? OMG Mommmm!!! something coming out of her nose...drooling ...ohh nooo....soooo wacky".

Devika pressed hard on the brake. Her eyes became bigger as she gave a fiery look to her son and whispered back "MANNERS, excuse me, I SAID MANNERS".

Platoon coiled back quickly sensing the danger. Rumelia giggled at the back seat and said "Aunty got nice big eyes, like Devi amma DURGA...... Malika said in a confident voice "She is Devi amma Durga,,, babyJan....Cant you see how she is protecting us?".......Devika took a deep breath in. Somehow she gets very uncomfortable with any compliments. She forgot how to take them gracefully.....gets flustered, as if she is never good enough for any compliment anymore.

She was driving home everybody in her SUV after picking up Platoon from school on her way from ER. Sanjay is out of town. She was just handling every difficult moment as it was coming to her. Suddenly her dull, boring life got intertw[1]ined with an unreal dramatic illness of a stranger. How she is going to protect this innocent vulnerable family? What's going to happen if the man dies tonight at ER? How she will handle the whole ominous event? Absolutely

---

[1] Durga! - The main Goddess in Hindu Religion with Ten hands; who creates heaven and destroy devils.

clueless..... she was driving only in seventy five miles/hr. Her mind was speeding in million miles/hr with big empty outer space of dark unknown and big asteroids were bouncing around like WHO, WHAT, HOW, WHY?

And mostly she was worried sick inside; just with the mere thought what Sanjay will say about this unreal saga? How stupid and un-sophisticated of Devika to get tangled in somebody else's business? He will yell …..WHY HER? WHY IT IS ALWAYS HER? Who invites trouble? She just could feel the future heat of the invisible anger on her back.

But in a strange way she is happy......deliriously, fervently happy secretly. After a long time she is in the front wheel. She is in charge of a very critical unknown situation. People are depending on her actions and judgement. like the way she used to take leadership ...to find a shortcut to bypass the furious mobs after Brigade meetings in Calcutta. Her friends were completely dependent on her rescue plans to reach home safe by crossing an inhuman, horrendous traffic jam in BIBADI BAG.

After leaving hospital she already contacted Malika and Rudra's families in India. Without knowing a single word of Telugu she managed to explain the situation by using Malika and Rumelia for translation.

She stopped at the ATM machine and got out three hundred dollar cash. She gave Malika the dollars now for emergency/ no question asked/ as Malika neither has ATM card, nor she knows Rudra's pin.

She stopped at the Krogger and got three big bottles of milk, five packs of bread, eighteen count egg cartons with few bundles of spinach and Dannon's fat free yogurt. No south-Indian family can survive too long without yogurt, she knows from her friends of Deshopriyo Park. At least a week's worth food is packed in her car for the family.

She asked and got a list of all Telugu friends they know here, and contacted few of them already to report the incidence in the office, at Rudra's work place. Telugu association was contacted and much to her surprise they were all willing to come even so late at night to help the family.

She sadly remembered that day she had labor pain and Sanjay was out of town…Ghosh da and boudi never picked up the phone…it went to answering machine fifteen times.

Soft rain was drizzling on the car window and little Rumelia just said " Daddy loves rain…. Mom …does he know its raining?" Malika was silent……a heavy metal jacket silence was suffocating every passengers in that lonely car moving in the darkness of doom. Platoon took out his favorite spongebob toy from his backpack and passed gently to Rumelia. His voice was soft, unusually kind… apologetic… "I think he knows its raining".

Chapter 7

The voice in the phone was heavy with accents, extra love for R's and T' s are kind of mixed with D' s. Mr. Ranganathan, Rudra's friend, was talking to Devika after three nightmarish days . "Mad(t)am…..you no worry….we a(R)e he(R)e besides YO….T(d)otally controlled(t) case….just tell us what(d) to d(t)o ".

Devika fumbled. If the case is totally controlled…why they are asking her? She did not say that she either has no clue. But she started talking. She said "I think someone should talk to the hospital administration. It's just not right to keep a man in a ventilator forever not knowing the progress".

Ranganathan blasted " HUNDRRED{t} percent Mad(t) am, the daily hospital bill is ve(a)rry cost(d)ly". Devika was thinking it should be probably wise to technically end this traumatic process by requesting to discontinue the ventilator. There is no way poor family or anybody else will be able to pay the bills. And this man is never going to be normal again as already probably brain dead. But Malika's face came up in her mind. Devika was silent for few awkward moments.

Malika goes to hospital religiously every day and night, leaving Rumelia with Devika. She got a bus pass from the social workers in the hospital. She has so much self-respect…..never asks for rides. She just sits in the ICU, wearing protective clothes, holding Rudra's hand, slowly massaging the fingers, one by one, and singing in a low tone like lullaby. She has her

Tirupati Locket which she touches to her husband's cold, immobile body. She speaks to her unconscious, semi-comatose husband about their village, the first day they met, how scared she was to ride the big jumbo jet coming to this country, how Rumelia is getting friendly with Platoon…like big brother and lil! sister……and sometimes she does not speaks at all….. she stares at Rudra's fixed expressionless open eyes …..…..and tears roll down from her eyes.

Nobody ever disturbs her. Not even the notorious ICU nurse managers. There is an untold support system going on in that small room where Philippinos, African Americans, Jamaicans, British …..Every nationalities and races bowed their heads to this rare scene of love and dedication of a little dark woman from India. They wrap blankets on her in the nights, bring her soups, escort her everywhere in the hospital, if nothing else…..just hold her hands…. cry with her….and pray together.

How Devika will even mention to her? About discontinuing ventilator? HOW? She felt she has two useless hands………as if no fingers on it. She placed the phone down.

Chapter 8

Dr. Martin was seating in his office turning his face to the bookshelf behind his computer terminal. As Devika entered he nodded to the other empty chair. She seated with caution as if seating on a chair made of glass, did not slump, stayed straight back. He looked typical six feet, blue eyed, silver-grey haired Caucasian male from UTAH or NEVADA, who are born with a plan to enroll in the army and later becomes either surgeon or anesthesiologist. The cold, crisp eyes reveal no emotion, each case is handled with rare perfection and every aspect of human life can be explained with anatomical details.

Devika started in a shy feeble voice, "Is there any hope that he can revive ?" "Of course! but the statistics are not so hot…only 17 % worldwide cases reported by WHO(world health org)……Do you take vitamins D ? I mean daily?"

Devika was perplexed and promptly said " No, I don't….but why ? How did you know?" He smiled like an innocent child. "Bad habits of a doctor, snooping for physical clues to search underlying cause. Sorry! You don't have to answer, but you can just take an extra strength Vit D pill once a week."

Devika got little bit more confidence. May be there is a human behind that astounding stature and overwhelming certificates and credentials hanging in the wall. She asked " So you think there is hope?"

"There is always hope. We physicians are just scratching the surfaces. Research proposed many new alternatives than traditional plasma exchange. There is a study recently in UK, Queen England Hospital about a new antigen Neurofascin, which is eliciting good outcome in one case".

Devika stood up and leaned on the table with excitement "So why are you not trying? Is that because of financial issues, the bills they could not pay to the hospital?"

His face turned red and stiff. He looked for two longest seconds thru Devika's eyes. It felt like a sharp electromagnetic wave passed thru her. The he stood up too. Leaning on the table, face to face with Devika and molten lava like words came out

"You have the audacity to come to my office and ask me that question ? You believe ?, HOW DARE YOU ? That I am holding myself from trying that therapy on your friend just because of hospital bills ? IN THE NAME OF HOLY SPIRIT, YOU DO HAVE GUTS…. But let me tell you something MISS JOAN OF ARK.. that's not how we practice medicine in this country. We treat everybody same…at least whatever resource we have…..otherwise your friend would have died in the first 48 hrs. Do you have any idea how much risk and malpractice problem I am diving into just even by mentioning the therapy? YOU DON'T I am SURE. YOU JUST think I am a leech sucking money out of the system for my personal gain?

DO you have any idea? A slightest one ? How hard a person has to work to become a hospitalist in this country? Endless exams, ten brutal years of our youth, thirty nine hours straight shifts without breaks, humiliation and insults of 4 gruesome residency years, Guillotine sharp loans hanging on our neck and patients and their relatives seeking miracle from misery….. unforgiving to the slightest error we make …AT LEAST errors we are eligible to make as human ? If you cannot TRUST us…AT least respect my courage, CAN YOU PLEASE?, I am taking this risk on me knowing fully well that if it does not work and had any bad outcomes your Lawyers and hospital administration is going to hang my burned bottoms at the front entrance of the hospital, HOW DARE YOU questioning my intentions ? GODDAMN it !! Let me tell you the fact MAM! I DON'T HAVE TO….I really don't have to try anything AT ALLL!!! I can just dump the case to Neurology and escape out of this sticky situation.

He was almost shaking with the violent anger….. "You know what ? YOU ARE EXACTLY RIGHT….why should I expect something different from somebody like you from underdeveloped country who thinks we are just money oriented brainless fat Americans without ETHICS . Fine…I will go by with your common sense, I will not try anything, FORGET IT…Why should I ? I don't have to, I have no responsibility, I COULD NOT CARE LESS!!!!"

Devika could not stand anymore. She had not slept or eaten properly for last few days, she was dizzy….but she smiled in confidence…she found the right Doctor….YES THERE IS HOPE…..There is DR. Martin. She smiled again and sat down on her knees…..tears rolling down from her eyes…and she said with her palms together as prayer " YOU HAVE to CARE, Who ? IF not YOU…..it was you who is wearing that white coat…..it was YOU WHO TOOK THE OATH, the promise, that you will try… I am from Calcutta, Mother Teresa's town . Mother said " Don't worry about numbers, just help one person, start with the person nearest at this time". Slowly a soft darkness swirled around her consciousness, everything was fading, phasing out slowly….she heard Dr. Martin asking for his nurse to call code blue, before everything became quiet and peaceful dark.

Chapter 9

She woke up slowly like a princess in a cushy pink chair at nurse's station, surrounded by eye glass wearing, confident, teddy bear like loving nurses. Dr. Martin was standing there like a tower of command and responsibility. He announced "Ok she is waking up, please check her blood sugar and another set of vitals please". He holds Devika's hand in a big, giant clasp and smiled "Don't worry I promise I will do my best for your friend Rudra, but you have to promise something to me too. Please DO NOT come to my office to argue about friend and PASS OUT on me. Oh God! You scared the hell out of all of us. Pheww!!! What a stubborn woman?...I admire your persistence. Make sure take your Irons and Vitamin D s before your next crusade". She laughed loud and so did everybody. Cassandra, the head nurse, gently took away the monitor and pulse ox from her hand and helped her to stand up.

The ride from the airport to home was strange. Sanjay was deadly quiet as she was pouring out her vivid experiences of last 6 days. She did not hide anything, for the first time in her life she was not timid or unsure. She was excited, enthusiastic as she told him how everybody chipped in. Dr. Martin's therapy worked wonder. Rudra opened his eyes and was able to speak some words. But most of his body is still immobile. Rudra's employer already provided fair share of the fund to pay for the special arrangement needed to make to transfer the family safely to back to India where rest of the treatment can take place in much lower cost and with massive family support.

She described in detail how this strange illness and doomed family story captured every media's attention. They story went live on local news channels, radio and social media. The story got published in local newspaper and whole town almost knows and embracing it. She did not skip the part that how desperately she approached even the CITY Mayor's office and they all agreed to support Rudra's case even though he is not a US citizen. He is a resident engineer who contributed in city's electrical corporation that was enough. Mayor's secretary took the initiative to raise money for the special medical flight that needs to be arranged that Rudra's body can stay in vertical position with a special medical team assisting the whole 22 hrs ride home. Good news that most of the funds are arranged but still there are lots needed to be done. She is calling all local Indian temples, volunteer organizations, Red Cross, everybody that whoever can help to raise money to pay the hospital bills and future treatment of this debilitating disease.

At home Platoon came running and gave Sanjay a big hug. Rumelia is standing shy in the corner. Sanjay raised his eyebrow and Devika explained "That's Malika's daughter Rumelia, her mom is in the hospital taking care of Daddy, so she stay with us and play with Platoon after school." Rudra said a dry, cold "hi" to her. And he straight went to the kitchen and poured himself a glass of water and ice. As Devika came in, he pulled out his purse and wrote a check of five hundred dollars and handed her. "You did great Devi! for saving someone's life. Here is my contribution."

Devika was speechless for few seconds. She just did not know how to accept this rare compliment. Her eyes became wet as she was approaching to say thank you and may be giving him a hug…..he stepped back. In a cold venomous icy tone he said "Exactly how many of my good friends you called? And begged for money? HOW MANY?" his voice was raising….. Platoon and Rumelia came running, astounded at the kitchen door….he continued…. "WHY you have to do this to me? Why you put my reputation and social status in danger….I am a respectable person here in the community, and YOU, MY WIFE, begging money for a complete stranger…somebody who we don't even know? Being a heroine…in social media? Saving someone's LIFE? At the cost of my reputation?"

His eyes were red, fingers pointed and he was practically yelling. Devika was standing there, falling back again in the same pit of insult, humiliation and worthlessness.…tears blinded her eyes, her face went down, all her enthusiasm was gone. Suddenly Platoon came inside the kitchen with big bold steps. He stood cross firm in the middle protecting Devika…and he yelled back, first time probably in his little 12 years of life "WHY ARE YOU MAKING MOMMY CRY? SHE DID A GOOD JOB……saving Rumelia's daddy. What happened if it was YOU WHO GOT SICK? If someone did not save YOUR life? If I have YOU in the hospital, Daddy? Tell me?…." He started sobbing.…and grabbed Devika's arm and pulled her away from the kitchen taking her to his playroom.

Sanjay stood there in total disbelief. Suddenly Platoon hit him with sharp arrows of light which refracted in his soul and he could see all seven colors of his attitude, selfishness, arrogance, bullying.… bright and shinning like a rainbow. He simply could not take it. The idea of if it was HIM in that dreary hospital bed, Devika and Platoon helpless on the street. He holds his balance by grabbing the refrigerator door. Then he heard the little sad voice of Rumelia…"Uncle, are you OK? Are you upset because of me? I know, I am not family, please let me stay with Aunty and Platoon dada…I will go away with DADDY in few days". Sanjay sat down on his knees on the floor and cried audibly like an inconsolable child, in front of her. Hugged her tight close to his chest, said in a very soft, confident voice "NO Rumelia, I am not upset with you…YOU WILL STAY WITH US…as long as needed. NO worry baby… YOU ARE FAMILY".

In his play room Platoon pulled out the YELLOWPAGE telephone book and gave it to Devika. He wipes her tears in small puffy hands and kissed her on forehead. And said "Mommy!!! Please don't be sad…JUST DON'T CALL DADDY's FRIENDS. There are other people…

people who may help us…let's call together". Like GOD listened to them…… a page with big letter P flipped out from that book. There were 348 entries for last name PATELS….. they started calling.

One by one.

Chapter 10

The AIRINDIA flight surprisingly was on time. Everything worked out smoothly. Malika and Rumelia were hugging Devika and Platoon every six minutes and crying. But nobody was sad. It was tears of joy. Tears of making impossible to possible by two insignificant housewives and two little kids. Felt like whole town was poured down at the waiting lobby, News channels, Mayor's office, Sentinel people, Cassandra, Dr. Martin's wife with big bouquet of flower, VA s in the wheelchairs….Motor cyclists, School teachers, Air hostesses, RUDRAs Telugu associations, Patel Brothers, Hindu temple, Red Cross, Shepherd's hope, Trinity church, Martha's soup kitchen… all colors, races, nationalities and beliefs were there….to cheer, celebrate and rejoice a rejuvenation. Boost up the courage and fighting spirit of an unknown little family. Everybody could relate and embraced the spirit of survival and just happy for the immortality of human will power. The plane went up like a red eagle soaring high in the deep, blue, clear sky, fearless, accelerating to reach the target. Everybody cheered, waving madly. Sanjay hugged Devika and Platoon and said "Let's go home."

After a long time they were so happy to be together. Laughing, joking, and listening to the music in the car. Platoon put his feet outside the back window. Sanjay did not even notice. He was holding Devika's hand the whole time and giving her the looks that he used to in first few precious weeks of their honeymoon. Devika was floating inside. Feeling giddy and empty at the same time. Like somebody removed a heavy concrete rock from her dull existence. Happiness is sprouting up like a rainbow fountain suddenly in the dark. Like she is watching the big fireworks bursting like shiny dandelions in the Fourth of July sky. After parking the car in the driveway she and Sanjay went inside. Platoon as usual ran to the mailbox. As Devika was pouring the Darjeeling tea in the bone china teapot, she heard Platoon's excited voice. "DAD, MOMMM…..look at this"….he came running inside the kitchen with dirty muddy shoes, his face red, sweaty and eyes were glistening like marbles. Holding high in his hand was an envelope, blue, soaked half in rain. Sanjay stopped at the bathroom door. "What is it? Platoon?"

Platoon said in an awestruck voice "An invitation from Mayor's office for MOM. They are going to give her some award. We are invited too as a family, DADDY? CAN WE PLEASSEEE ALL GO? WE MUST DADDY".

The pale orange light of a happy afternoon drifted in the room softly correcting all significant errors and clumsiness of the past. Sanjay looked at his wife's unsure, perplexed, anxious face…..as if time have stopped for few silent seconds… seeking apology…seeking permission for a housewife to celebrate an unusual event of saving a life. Sanjay took few long strides to cross the living room, lifted Devika high up in the air with full embrace circling her waist and said "OFCOURSE PLATOON! WE ALL GO. Mommy is so special".

Devika changed four times. Clothes were piled as heap at the master bedroom floor. She could not decide whether she wear Indian dress or just casual American clothes, or just a salwar kurta…or just that stupid black suit she bought one time while interviewing for jobs. The day she got appointment letter pregnancy test was positive. The dress was hanging since then in her closet. Never used. She is watching her solid legs and wondering whether she will at all fit in her old black stockings. Sanjay came in with his perfect still grey suit with a white cheerful polka dot satin tie. He smelled rich cologne and looked so young and happy, humming Godfather soundtrack tunes. He said "Devi we are getting late. Hurry up baby. Wear that white silk with burgundy border. And that artistic nose thing your Mom gave you. "

Devika half shouted in disbelief" Are you insane? A nose ring in Mayor's office? That will be so tacky and ridiculous". Sanjay went out to the driveway and said aloud, "Fifteen more min, that's all you got. We got to move, Hurry up Devi!"

Platoon was watching half of his mouth open from the upper seating benches of the auditorium. Devika was standing in the middle of the stage. Auditorium was full with people that they barely know. Mayor approached Devika with a golden key almost three ft. long, beautifully curved and handed her with a huge plated certificate. He said in microphone "Devika you are awarded "THE GOLDEN RESIDENT AWARD" of our town for being so brave and selfless to save someone's life. This is the key of our town. You will keep it always as a memento of your noble work and unifying all of us to save a family, to save a little girl's daddy. You are hour RESIDENT of the YEAR. Everybody stood up, cheering, national anthems, both American and Indian was playing, Devika was holding that key confidently across her chest, her face shining and confident with pride. Suddenly confetti, multicolored, with golden stripes fell from overhead as a surprise gift, showering her.

Platoon watched with awe…..suddenly it felt the DURGAPUJA DAY……Drums are beating fast, the smoke of dhup dhuno illuminating the holy canvass, RED vermilions all over, his MOM standing in a red border sari, with a golden trishul in her hand, SHINING CHAINED NOSERING….she can destroy the demon, she can rebuild the heaven…. as if Priest dadu is chanting in his baritone voice "YA DEVI SORBOVUTESHU….SHAKTIRUPENO SANGSSTITHA, Nomostossoi…NAMO, NAMO!!!. He shivered in excitement and grabbed Sanjay's arm whispering "BABA……never call her HOUSEWIFE again when you are angry, she looks like MA DUGGA baba. Just like MA DUGGA". Sanjay enveloped him with two loving arms and whispered back "I am so sorry BABAN….I will never…I promise you… SHE IS MA DUGGA".

END

10 exciting weeks writing Housewife

Chapter 1

Today I am starting my first chronical story Housewife. Why did I choose the title? I have very little experience in this role. I could not spend too much time home as I had to go through a very extensive school/work/professional life. But with great helplessness and respect, I watched the life of my most intelligent, kind hearted, well educated, beautiful friends spending their lives in this hardest job in the world. There are almost no vacation, no sick leaves, no gratuity, no raise, and few if any "Thank you". There is no special work related visa, no Medicare, no organizations to seek support. But a very steep curve to rise and acute responsibility to raise the children, our next generation to become the most valuable citizens of the future. All the valedictorians, principals honor roles, spelling bee stars, ballerinas, national debaters, behind all of them ....endless toils and silent sacrifices of all personal degrees, hobbies, passions, many more from a woman in shadow. Devika, my heroine is one of them. Let's read her story.....let's find the strength and endurance that hold our society together...a strength and will power of a HOUSEWIFE

Chapter 2

Housewife/ Chapter two/ Day two.....Story continued.......as we ended: Devika sat up quickly, Her Monday begun......

Chapter 3

Story continues: 303 people engaged , reading, reacting yesterday.......as we said.....Devika still drinks coffee ...like before when she feels down........read more CLLIMMMAXXXX TODAY. HOUSEWIFE CHAPTER 3

Chapter 4

Posting 4th chapter today brings out mixed feelings. Unbelievable response from readers, 1046 reads so far in only 3 days. Feeling lucky and blessed. But at the same time someone wrote "We all are engrossed and enjoying...but letting you know privately" Should I be sad? Or just be reassured? that the story actually went deeper than I intended and touched some precious inner feelings... so I bow to you all, letting me be the storyteller....and I continue to write the story of DEVIKA, the unusual brave HOUSEWIFE

Chapter 5

Sincerely sorry for dozing off last night after charts. Missed posting chapter 5. Goodness gracious....92 angry mails in my box at AM ? WHAT HAPPENED TO DEVIKA? YOU CANT STOP now!!!!.....ok ok kkkkk...sorryyy...and a very humble sweet and sad letter made my day "Amrita darun laglo. ETAI bastov. Amra nari swadhinota niye joto I chitkar korina keno ....Etai sotti. Sudhu house wife noy, working women der obosthao khub subidher noy re. Sob samle Jodi chakri korte paro to koro, otherwise big NO, bari te Jodi salary tar financial dorkar na thake....tahole to aro kom support pawa jay". Sat quietly few minutes......never realized so much pain and love is possible ...had to come out...just by writing an insignificant story. So here it is......

Chapter 6.

Not much intro tonite….just wrote

Chapter 7

Personal note: With Daughter's exam, Huby out of town, charts, grocery, Sunday laundry, cooking, Monday preps......I never thought I will be able to write chapter 7 tonight. But I could.......because of my lovely avid readers and supporters.....KUDOS to my team... and here it's ...my humble story telling.. goes on ...as 3077 people reached my story in 1 week.

Chapter 8

Woke up midnight and with utmost joy...today 5000 people reached my story.....gives me courage to go on....so I write the story of Devika... she went to see Dr. Martin

CHAPTER 9

Love comes in form of complains. I got 213 in my inbox...as I am late posting my chapter 9. Apology from heart. I am honored to be your storyteller...your eagerness is my fuel....So I continued...DEVIKAS story

Chapter10.

Closing a two weeks memorable roller coaster ride with my story was not easy. I humbly touched 7000 readers for m y humble story of Devika. Housewife. Tears of joy in my eyes too that I could complete my work. The last and final chapter 10 tonight. Thanks for all your unconditional love and support. It's really hard to let Devika go. She became so real.

Prologue

Independence Day is the story of journey to our basics. Going back to the roots. Cherishing the memory and indispensible learning we got from amazing teachers from post independence era. Who hold strong to their principle and beliefs. No hooligans could scare them or deviate them from the basic role models as a teacher. In today's world of lost faith and ambience of hypocrisy, this was a rare opportunity for us to go back and salute our teachers, our heroes.

Dedicated to my all my teachers who taught me to stand up for truth

Independence Day

Amrita Mukherjee

The phone was ringing…..she could hear,… even standing in shower, early morning, dove soap foams, orange towel , hot steam, regular setting of a working day….routine. She never carries her android in bathroom, fear of dropping it in unspeakable water. She must have left it on kitchen counter. Must be her Mom calling from India, who has an unfailing aptitude of calling her while she is in shower. Predictable old lady, AKA, Mrs. Hitler….maintains her regime and rules. Mom will never change. She sighed and stopped the water faucet.

Boom, boom…knock on the bathroom door, "call from India, it's for u MOM"….small brown hand holding the phone came thru bathroom door, slammed the machine on marble sink…. door wide open….gone. Rohana is 10, cart and brief, knows her priorities….like catching school bus in 8 min. She can hear her thumping upstairs, frantically looking last min items for school.

Awkwardly she picked the phone carefully avoided drenching in still dripping water from hand and hair. It was a different voice than her MOM, with heavy accents and unsure muffled tone. It was Mrs. Banerjee, the principal of her elementary school. She was addressing her, with the full, formal name that she does not use anymore. America snipped it 20 years ago in a shorter, cuter version. She was inviting her to visit the school on 15th August, the Independence Day celebration. To raise the flag as an ex-student. Of course, her mother told the principal that she is coming home during that time. News awaited to be published as the most significant news in local newspaper probably with innate advertising skill of her MOM.

She was uneasy to commit to such an honor, standing in soaked towel in a hazy bathroom. She managed "I will try my best". Mrs. Banerjee said "You must, children are waiting to see you". She said children…….not kids. Some static sound caught in and phone went silent. She stood there confused. A bit numb, looking at the middle aged lumpy face in a semi lucent mirror. How this face is going to be suitable for such an honor?

The whole day while dealing with nausea, vomiting, fever, sore throat, depression and rectal abscess cases of her patients, she was distracted. Thinking of the school. A small red building with green gate. Right across from her old house that they lived when Dad was alive. Lined with serene eucalyptus trees. A big Banyan tree at the back yard, with hanging roots, that they used to swing like mini Tarzans. The math teacher, Parul Miss, drawing class. The bellman Volada. Those starchy uniforms with white shirt and blue skirt, tight banana pleat hairstyles with blue ribbons. Once she fell down and broke her elbow from slides, and how scary was it when a snake came inside the classroom during monsoon season.

Memories were coming like gentle spring rain, showering her with nameless emotions. Long forgotten. Suddenly found. So precious to loose…but too far to embrace. On her way home, driving, she was happy, humming the school prayer song, dhono dhanye pushpe vora. A rare smile flushed her face like soft afterglow.

At dinner Rohanas Dad announced "You may have to give a speech. I thought you are never comfortable doing that.". She protested, passing the breads, "They said only flag, no speech". He smiled his confident, all proof smile. "You better have one ready". Johana clapped " Ooops, Mom is going to look so funny……ha ha giving speeches." Kids can say cruel, insensitive things at this age. She was cutting her salads but her mind drifted. Seriously, what if they need her to speak. The whole idea runs a sharp chill down her spine.

On the long 16 hr flight from Chicago to Delhi she scribbled at least 13 prospective speeches and liked none. She kept throwing them in mashed paper ball with leftover, tasteless food tray. She was thinking maybe it's a good idea to just quit the whole celebration. But the school was sending strange unseen magnetic vibes, hard to ignore, rising urge to run and see her old classrooms, the playground and the new kids. The soft fleshy red banyan fruits…..they used make fake strings to decorate each other.

Night before the celebration she said she is not going while eating dinner with her Mom in that same old wobbly three legged table. Her Mom raised her famous Bollywood, 45 degree angled, Nargis eyebrows and demanded " Just because you are afraid of giving speeches ? I thought you are brave, dissecting dead bodies in the midnight lab while in med school. What is wrong with your generation? No sense of respect or responsibility to the place which gave you first education?" Mom can still make someone so humiliated and inspire to do something unusual at the same time. Amazing grace she preserved at age 79.

So she went. The gate was open and kids were playing all over. Innocent faced blue, white uniform clad angels. The flag stand covered with fresh flower, incense burning. New teachers busy arranging chairs. She took a deep breath. The banyan tree is still there although looks much smaller. Her classrooms are now looks old, with futile effort to leftover repainting job. Marks of bad maintenance and molding on walls. She was taken inside the office. This is the place only once she entered as a student…..when a classmate boy poked her eyes with sharp metal scale. The old principal called them both and after their spills, the boy got beaten. Straight, simple and effective.

And all of a sudden she saw that chair. A small old brown one. Flashing memories came back. The most important day of her five years of elementary education. The principal was tied with rope and being insulted and humiliated by some local, political gundas. They were threatening him to burn alive; ominous kerosene can under the chair. They were dangling the matchsticks. Female teachers were crying loud, all scared, afraid, confused pandemonium. Each moment of, anxiety, fear and impending doom came back…….27 years ago….but crystal clear in her memory. Amongst all bewilderment, frantic run around frenzies…..Principal stayed calm. He said "Go ahead, burn me, before you can burn my school, or touch my students". He was originally from Bangladesh, Dhaka, a stubborn so called "bangal" who had seen war, riot and a divided nation.

She stood there, looking at the chair in silence. Slowly something arisen in her mind, a feeling so strong, unknown, somewhat like confidence. She was not nervous anymore. She found her answer. After a while when they invited her to the program at flag stand and requested her to speak to the students she was not afraid. She confidently walked to the microphone and said "Hello everybody! I was told to speak about independence, our story of great brave shahids who made it possible 68 yrs ago. But I am going to talk about my Principal, who was in this school long time ago and taught me bravery, the right to protest injustice and true meaning of Independence … .. everybody was riveted, listening…a soft rainbow came out fighting monsoon sky…..students were liking the unusual story…..even the father of a fifth grader….standing far in the school gate….who tried to pierce her eyes with sharp metal scale 27 years ago.

END

Comments for Independence Day

A crisp journey down the memory lane, a rare tribute towards that other age, postindepence when undaunted souls resisted wrongdoers, ideal teachers building trustful students, most unlike the opportunistic present time.

Very good work as the first story. Keep it up.

Comments for
Independence Day

Very nicely written! Travelled to my childhood school while reading

Cant believe a story can be so simple. No pretense

Story is at the core. Close to all our heart

A story made me cry. Made an effort to go back to my school and it was precious.

All by anonymous

Prologue of Critical Connoisseur:

This is a story of an unusual romance. A critical person who is generally misunderstood by average population. A disorganized girl, happy go lucky, generally stamped as weird by commonality. A person who loves Mathematics. Another person who loves to talk about movies. A person knows intricate details of Bengali cooking. A reckless woman who does not have a clue about culinary science. They meet in a September afternoon across an insignificant table of a studio apartment.

Discover the magic afterwards.

Dedicated to my loving husband Aniket Bhattacharya

Critical Connoisseur

Amrita Mukherjee

Rohit is famous/ infamous for his passion for food. Like a Maestro in picking his violin or choosing the right chord while playing. He exactly knows the taste of lentil soup and how it can be spoiled if lavished with garlic. In his opinion garlic should be banned from most Bengali cuisines due to its raw sexual flavour. It kills the soft intellectual delicacy of a dish much like an aggressive lover who does not care much for foreplay.

He is a living terror in his Bengali boudi circle unknowingly. His sharp criticism and detail discussion to improve the quality of rasmalai and how sour cream cannot be a replacement of true badam gravy in a fish curry runs cold sweats of embarrassment and fear among newly married Calcutta boudis in his small town. People think twice and revise their menu carefully before inviting Rohit. It's a small town with few Bengali families in a cold North American city. Who wants to be rude enough not to include a bachelor in a scrumptious Bengali dinner?

Nobody does. But then Rohit is fastidious.

Compared to his male friends, Rohit is completely oblivious to stock market and contemporary political gossips of USA or Indo-American business relationship. He fails to buzz to American beer or long legs of shorts' clad females or even bridge games. He like three things in life: mathematics, talking about his Presidency college friends and perfect Bengali food, unadulterated, with affluent USA, Wal-Mart/Target derived ingredients.

His tea still gets shipped from Calcutta Subodh's shop carefully chosen by his brother every month; a combination of half dust and half leaf cautiously packaged in a five layers internationally protected materials, lest it loses its aroma. The sight of it lightens up Rohit's face better than any prospective date. Rohit has fifteen bone china teapots in his kitchen with immaculate silver spoons collected from around the world to brew his Darjeeling tea. It is obvious that he carries a stopwatch to brew his tea exactly two minutes with boiling hot water, before mixing his splenda or cream. And serving cups has to be pre washed with boiled water to retain the warmth and sustain the flavour. You have to be completely out of your mind to offer Rohit a cup of so-called nauseatingly sweet, boiled, masala tea; popular in general desi gatherings. He would distastefully decline it and provide a short, fifteen minutes lecture about the absolute lack of sophistication to offer that kinda tea for him.

No wonder he is still happily bachelor at age of 35 and enjoying every moment of his idiosyncratic freedom with his strange habits of making four eggs omelettes with fried onion and green chili with dash of cilantro at 2:00 AM in the night with crisp golden toasts with butter. In the background he likes to have Bilayet Khan's sitar and writes his calculation with a terrific speed that matches with the jhala beats of sitar.

So Rohit was not sure that morning. Whether to go or not? It's the magic September month in Washington DC. Crisp fall wind had blown over the Potomac River and crossing the Georgetown bridge. Maple leaves are pompously flying in the wind, their orange and deep yellow colour, reminding one of an apricot topping of a crisp croissant. Smiles are abundant and contagious, music in every corner of The GWU campus and the black guy gave him a dollar discount before handing over the yellow rose bouquet as he came out of Foggy Bottom subway. It's one of the scrupulous plans of Raina.

"Please Rohit", she begged over the phone, "Go meet the girl".

Rohit feels disgusted with a big D every time his cousin sister pulls this prank on him. Actually Raina is a very sensible woman, an economics lecturer at Columbia University with two kids and a stable, somewhat roundish hubby with poor sense of humour. They are the only family member close by and Raina still believes, one day, Rohit will find the magic girl who will fulfil every obtuse and acute angle of his critical imagination.

Raina also has a soft point, a different respect for Rohit. Two years ago Raina had a nasty fight with her hubby and left NY by Greyhound bus with two kids and a suitcase. Rohit did not ask a single question, checked himself out in a hotel and left the house for Raina to be alone for two whole days, hysterically shaking and crying and finally calming down. He took the kids to a NASA visit. Not a single soul had known. Not even Rania's parents. She went back NY happily with Raj and made up sweetly ever after. Only Rohit could keep such a secret and can deal a crisis with a rare strength.

So the plan unfolded again for Rohit.

"Come on Bhaiya, she is very intellectual, a GWU Masters' student, lives right across from Gelman Library on H street; just see her and say I gave you this packet to hand her."

"How does she look?"

"Funny, a bit shorty, laughs a lot, speaks Bengali, Yes ! Yes! Not anglicised…..no memsahib. Also I heard she is interested in experimental cooking".

At this point Rohit slammed down the phone and decided he will go.

"What the hell is experimental cooking?" he mumbled to himself as he was shaving looking at his moustache in the mirror. He spared the moustache this time for no good reason. "Either you know or you don't know cooking….the experimental is just a bull crap in between, Huhh!!!"

The stairs were curved and a musty smells of curry signalling the existence of many desi students' here, some lounging outside the porch like a no different Calcuttan rock. Apt 501, a dark brown door, opened ajar, a strange smell of burnt cinnamon and half cooked shrimp coming through the door. Rohit held his breath. It's probably not too late to turn back and pretend that he never came. But too late…..a chubby face with a turquoise scarf came out, a yellow stained spoon in one hand…..

"Oh hello??? Come on in", the girl said in a high pitched voice.

Rohit realized that he is actually smiling, extending the rose bouquet properly which is not so Rohit at all. The girl took it instantly and opened the door widely with a smile as if she knew Rohit since kindergarten. So vibrant and heart-warming!

"OMG, I was so nervous all morning, Raina told me you are a great cook and does not like hanky panky when it comes cooking. OMG you not going to believe this I got Tiger Shrimps from Potomac river front and all the cook books of Madhur Zaffrey. I been cooking for the last hour… but somehow it smells weird. Come on in, please have a seat", she went on.

In all this torrential waves of laughter, smell and conversation Rohit noticed there is a fine piece of shrimp shell, still hanging on her dark black wavy curly hair and she has a small black mole on her left upper lip.

She was constantly talking, moving, pouring sangria in a coffee cup; "sorry! I don't have goblets. Do you like tuna sandwiches? I just brought it, as a contingency plan, in case you can't eat my menu. Ha ha ha ……in the last party everybody got sick after eating my carrot skin desert. But please don't worry! I did not cook that today…."

"And what do you think about Vikram Seth, oh!! I cannot believe how popular he is among my Trinidad friends and guess what my friend Damini found a ticket of only 700 dollar at Tarom Airlines, going Calcutta thru Rumania, and don't tell me you never tried the egg rolls at Gariahat", she went on smoothly like a caramel ice cream sliding from one topic to the other.

All Rohit could do was to look and look and smile occasionally. He was curious. Something unknown, unpredictable, changing dimensions, liquid crystallography almost making him attracted…interested….after a long, long time ….some thing new….

Finally she put the bowl on the table and so eagerly asked Rohit, "OMG try it…. Do you need an extra fork ?

"Oh! Why not ? Certainly."

Rohit tried very carefully not to be sarcastic or rude. He started eating cautiously and digging the black, gelatinous material in the bowl….more he digs…the worse it became … finally he got exhausted…..dropped his fork and blurted out rather indignantly "where are the shrimps? It tastes like sea weed in a cinnamon broth".

She was quiet. First time in last two hours…. like suddenly she realized……her eyes stopped dancing……she looked down and said sadly, "I am so sorry…..I am no cook….I just did all these hula hooo to impress you…….Raina told me……Please ignore this".

She puts down her head completely hiding between two small palms……..on the table.

It was a strange afternoon, autumn lights with its orange hue filtering through lace curtains and flooding that insignificant table of Apt# 501 between two strangers.

It was a September afternoon…..and seating there Rohit did the most un-Rohitly act of his life. He softly touched her hair to pick out the shrimp shell and could manage to say "Please don't fret……I guess, I will do the cooking……..do you know how to do the dishes?"

END

Author Biography

Amrita was born as a fourth daughter of an engineer in a small industrial town of Durgapur, West Bengal, India. As she lost her father at a very young age, she grew up in an unconventional all women household of 1970's patriarchal Indian society.

Her passion for art and literature bloomed in those early years when she was studying Botany, with Biochemistry major at Santiniketan, Visvabharati.

She came to USA at tender age of twenty two as a student at The George Washington University, School of Engineering and Applied Science and completed her MS in 1997. Her career started as a System Analyst at General Motors/EDS.

Fate took its evil turn and at a critical juncture of her personal life, Amrita embraced Medical School at an advanced age. She passed with flying colors with best research award with the graduating class of 2008 from NSUCOM/ Florida.

Today Amrita lives in Orlando, Florida, being a dedicated Physician of homeless people in an underserved community. Amrita loves to go to mission trips in places like Peru and Africa. She has a daughter and her husband, who is constantly supporting her personal and professional development.

Amrita writes her stories, amazing milestones of her past, that she crossed as an Indian female immigrant in a foreign land and hopes that it will inspire many to fight their odds and enjoy the magic of survival.

Please send your thoughts and suggestions to AUTHOR at Amritascreativity@gmail.com.

Printed in the United States
By Bookmasters